D0292215

THE BEATRIX POTTER COLLECTION

MOUSE TALES

Four Original Peter Rabbit Stories

THE ORIGINAL AND AUTHORIZED EDITIONS

BY BEATRIX POTTER

TM

New colour reproductions

FREDERICK WARNE

Published by the Penguin Group
27 Wrights Lane, London W8 5TZ, England
Viking Penguin Inc., 40 West 23rd Street, New York, New York 10010, USA
Penguin Books Australia Ltd, Ringwood, Victoria, Australia
Penguin Books Canada Ltd, 2801 John Street, Markham, Ontario, Canada L3R 1B4
Penguin Books (NZ) Ltd, 182–190 Wairau Road, Auckland 10, New Zealand

Penguin Books Ltd, Registered Offices: Harmondsworth, Middlesex, England

First published in this edition 1989

1 3 5 7 9 10 8 6 4 2

ISBN 0 7232 3543 0

Typeset, printed and bound in Great Britain by
William Clowes Limited, Beccles and London

Contents

THE TALE OF
TWO BAD MICE

ONCE upon a time there was a very beautiful doll's-house; it was red brick with white windows, and it had real muslin curtains and a front door and a chimney.

IT belonged to two Dolls called Lucinda and Jane, at least it belonged to Lucinda, but she never ordered meals.

Jane was the Cook; but she never did any cooking, because the dinner had been bought ready-made, in a box full of shavings.

THERE were two red lobsters and a ham, a fish, a pudding, and some pears and oranges.

They would not come off the plates, but they were extremely beautiful.

ONE morning Lucinda and Jane had gone out for a drive in the doll's perambulator. There was no one in the nursery, and it was very quiet. Presently there was a little scuffling, scratching noise in a corner near the fire-place, where there was a hole under the skirting-board.

Tom Thumb put out his head for a moment, and then popped it in again.

Tom Thumb was a mouse.

A MINUTE afterwards, Hunca Munca, his wife, put her head out, too; and when she saw that there was no one in the nursery, she ventured out on the oilcloth under the coalbox.

THE doll's-house stood at the other side of the fire-place. Tom Thumb and Hunca Munca went cautiously across the hearthrug. They pushed the front door—it was not fast.

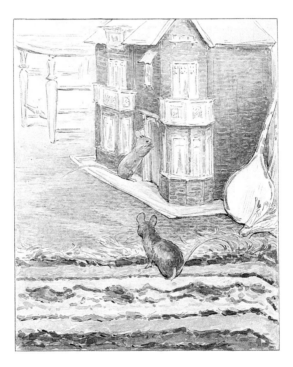

TOM THUMB and Hunca Munca went upstairs and peeped into the dining-room. Then they squeaked with joy!

Such a lovely dinner was laid out upon the table! There were tin spoons, and lead knives and forks, and two dolly-chairs—all *so* convenient!

13

TOM THUMB set to work at once
to carve the ham. It was a beautiful
shiny yellow, streaked with red.

The knife crumpled up and hurt
him; he put his finger in his mouth.

'It is not boiled enough; it is hard.
You have a try, Hunca Munca.'

H UNCA MUNCA stood up in her chair, and chopped at the ham with another lead knife.

'It's as hard as the hams at the cheesemonger's,' said Hunca Munca.

THE ham broke off the plate with a jerk, and rolled under the table.

'Let it alone,' said Tom Thumb; 'give me some fish, Hunca Munca!'

HUNCA MUNCA tried every tin spoon in turn; the fish was glued to the dish.

Then Tom Thumb lost his temper. He put the ham in the middle of the floor, and hit it with the tongs and with the shovel—bang, bang, smash, smash!

The ham flew all into pieces, for underneath the shiny paint it was made of nothing but plaster!

THEN there was no end to the rage and disappointment of Tom Thumb and Hunca Munca. They broke up the pudding, the lobsters, the pears and the oranges.

As the fish would not come off the plate, they put it into the red-hot crinkly paper fire in the kitchen; but it would not burn either.

TOM THUMB went up the kitchen chimney and looked out at the top—there was no soot.

WHILE Tom Thumb was up the chimney, Hunca Munca had another disappointment. She found some tiny canisters upon the dresser, labelled—Rice—Coffee—Sago—but when she turned them upside down, there was nothing inside except red and blue beads.

THEN those mice set to work to do all the mischief they could—especially Tom Thumb! He took Jane's clothes out of the chest of drawers in her bedroom, and he threw them out of the top floor window.

But Hunca Munca had a frugal mind. After pulling half the feathers out of Lucinda's bolster, she remembered that she herself was in want of a feather bed.

WITH Tom Thumb's assistance she carried the bolster downstairs, and across the hearthrug. It was difficult to squeeze the bolster into the mouse-hole; but they managed it somehow.

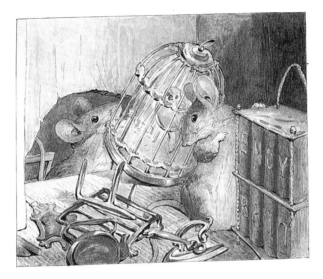

THEN Hunca Munca went back
and fetched a chair, a book-case, a
bird-cage, and several small odds and
ends. The book-case and the bird-cage
refused to go into the mouse-hole.

HUNCA MUNCA left them behind the coal-box, and went to fetch a cradle.

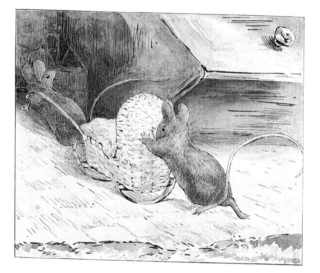

HUNCA MUNCA was just return-
ing with another chair, when suddenly there was a noise of talking
outside upon the landing. The mice
rushed back to their hole, and the dolls
came into the nursery.

WHAT a sight met the eyes of Jane and Lucinda! Lucinda sat upon the upset kitchen stove and stared; and Jane leant against the kitchen dresser and smiled—but neither of them made any remark.

THE book-case and the bird-cage
were rescued from under the coal-
box—but Hunca Munca has got the
cradle, and some of Lucinda's clothes.

SHE also has some useful pots and
pans, and several other things.

THE little girl that the doll's-house
belonged to, said,—'I will get a
doll dressed like a policeman!'

BUT the nurse said,—'I will set a mouse-trap!'

SO that is the story of the two Bad Mice,—but they were not so very very naughty after all, because Tom Thumb paid for everything he broke.

He found a crooked sixpence under the hearthrug; and upon Christmas Eve, he and Hunca Munca stuffed it into one of the stockings of Lucinda and Jane.

A ND very early every morning—
before anybody is awake—Hunca
Munca comes with her dust-pan and
her broom to sweep the Dollies' house!

THE TALE OF
JOHNNY TOWN~MOUSE

JOHNNY TOWN-MOUSE was born in a cupboard. Timmy Willie was born in a garden. Timmy Willie was a little country mouse who went to town by mistake in a hamper. The gardener sent vegetables to town once a week by carrier; he packed them in a big hamper.

THE gardener left the hamper by
the garden gate, so that the carrier
could pick it up when he passed.
Timmy Willie crept in through a hole
in the wicker-work, and after eating
some peas—Timmy Willie fell fast
asleep.

HE awoke in a fright, while the hamper was being lifted into the carrier's cart. Then there was a jolting, and a clattering of horse's feet; other packages were thrown in; for miles and miles—jolt—jolt—jolt! and Timmy Willie trembled amongst the jumbled up vegetables.

AT last the cart stopped at a house, where the hamper was taken out, carried in, and set down. The cook gave the carrier sixpence; the back door banged, and the cart rumbled away. But there was no quiet; there seemed to be hundreds of carts passing. Dogs barked; boys whistled in the street; the cook laughed, the parlour maid ran up and down-stairs; and a canary sang like a steam engine.

TIMMY WILLIE, who had lived all his life in a garden, was almost frightened to death. Presently the cook opened the hamper and began to unpack the vegetables. Out sprang the terrified Timmy Willie.

UP jumped the cook on a chair, exclaiming 'A mouse! a mouse! Call the cat! Fetch me the poker, Sarah!' Timmy Willie did not wait for Sarah with the poker; he rushed along the skirting board till he came to a little hole, and in he popped.

HE dropped half a foot, and crashed into the middle of a mouse dinner party, breaking three glasses.—'Who in the world is this?' inquired Johnny Town-mouse. But after the first exclamation of surprise he instantly recovered his manners.

WITH the utmost politeness he introduced Timmy Willie to nine other mice, all with long tails and white neck-ties. Timmy Willie's own tail was insignificant. Johnny Town-mouse and his friends noticed it; but they were too well bred to make personal remarks; only one of them asked Timmy Willie if he had ever been in a trap?

44

THE dinner was of eight courses; not much of anything, but truly elegant. All the dishes were unknown to Timmy Willie, who would have been a little afraid of tasting them; only he was very hungry, and very anxious to behave with company manners. The continual noise upstairs made him so nervous, that he dropped a plate. 'Never mind, they don't belong to us,' said Johnny.

'WHY don't those youngsters come back with the dessert?' It should be explained that two young mice, who were waiting on the others, went skirmishing upstairs to the kitchen between courses. Several times they had come tumbling in, squeaking and laughing; Timmy Willie learnt with horror that they were being chased by the cat. His appetite failed, he felt faint. 'Try some jelly?' said Johnny Town-mouse.

'NO? Would you rather go to bed? I will show you a most comfortable sofa pillow.'

The sofa pillow had a hole in it. Johnny Town-mouse quite honestly recommended it as the best bed, kept exclusively for visitors. But the sofa smelt of cat. Timmy Willie preferred to spend a miserable night under the fender.

IT was just the same next day. An excellent breakfast was provided—for mice accustomed to eat bacon; but Timmy Willie had been reared on roots and salad. Johnny Town-mouse and his friends racketted about under the floors, and came boldly out all over the house in the evening. One particularly loud crash had been caused by Sarah tumbling downstairs with the tea-tray; there were crumbs and sugar and smears of jam to be collected, in spite of the cat.

TIMMY WILLIE longed to be at
home in his peaceful nest in a
sunny bank. The food disagreed with
him; the noise prevented him from
sleeping. In a few days he grew so
thin that Johnny Town-mouse noticed
it, and questioned him. He listened to
Timmy Willie's story and inquired
about the garden. 'It sounds rather a
dull place? What do you do when it
rains?'

49

'WHEN it rains, I sit in my little sandy burrow and shell corn and seeds from my Autumn store. I peep out at the throstles and blackbirds on the lawn, and my friend Cock Robin. And when the sun comes out again, you should see my garden and the flowers—roses and pinks and pansies— no noise except the birds and bees, and the lambs in the meadows.'

'THERE goes that cat again!' exclaimed Johnny Town-mouse. When they had taken refuge in the coal-cellar, he resumed the conversation; 'I confess I am a little disappointed; we have endeavoured to entertain you, Timothy William.'

'Oh yes, yes, you have been most kind; but I do feel so ill,' said Timmy Willie.

'IT may be that your teeth and digestion are unaccustomed to our food; perhaps it might be wiser for you to return in the hamper.'

'Oh? Oh!' cried Timmy Willie.

'Why of course for the matter of that we could have sent you back last week,' said Johnny rather huffily—'did you not know that the hamper goes back empty on Saturdays?'

SO Timmy Willie said goodbye to his new friends, and hid in the hamper with a crumb of cake and a withered cabbage leaf; and after much jolting, he was set down safely in his own garden.

SOMETIMES on Saturdays he went
to look at the hamper lying by the
gate, but he knew better than to get
in again. And nobody got out, though
Johnny Town-mouse had half promised
a visit.

THE winter passed; the sun came out again; Timmy Willie sat by his burrow warming his little fur coat and sniffing the smell of violets and spring grass. He had nearly forgotten his visit to town. When up the sandy path all spick and span with a brown leather bag came Johnny Town-mouse!

TIMMY WILLIE received him
with open arms. 'You have come
at the best of all the year, we will
have herb pudding and sit in the sun.'

'H'm'm! it is a little damp,' said
Johnny Town-mouse, who was carrying
his tail under his arm, out of the mud.

'WHAT is that fearful noise?' he started violently.

'That?' said Timmy Willie, 'that is only a cow; I will beg a little milk, they are quite harmless, unless they happen to lie down upon you. How are all our friends?'

JOHNNY'S account was rather middling. He explained why he was paying his visit so early in the season; the family had gone to the seaside for Easter; the cook was doing spring cleaning, on board wages, with particular instructions to clear out the mice. There were four kittens, and the cat had killed the canary.

'THEY say we did it; but I know better,' said Johnny Town-mouse. 'Whatever is that fearful racket?'

'That is only the lawn-mower; I will fetch some of the grass clippings presently to make your bed. I am sure you had better settle in the country, Johnny.'

'H'M 'M—we shall see by Tuesday week; the hamper is stopped while they are at the sea-side.'

'I am sure you will never want to live in town again,' said Timmy Willie.

BUT he did. He went back in the very next hamper of vegetables; he said it was too quiet !!

ONE place suits one person, another place suits another person. For my part I prefer to live in the country, like Timmy Willie.

The Tale of
Mrs. Tittlemouse

ONCE upon a time there was a wood-mouse, and her name was Mrs. Tittlemouse.

She lived in a bank under a hedge.

SUCH a funny house! There were yards and yards of sandy passages, leading to storerooms and nut-cellars and seed-cellars, all amongst the roots of the hedge.

THERE was a kitchen, a parlour, a pantry, and a larder.

Also, there was Mrs. Tittlemouse's bedroom, where she slept in a little box bed!

MRS. TITTLEMOUSE was a most terribly tidy particular little mouse, always sweeping and dusting the soft sandy floors.

Sometimes a beetle lost its way in the passages.

'Shuh! Shuh! little dirty feet!' said Mrs. Tittlemouse, clattering her dustpan.

AND one day a little old woman
ran up and down in a red spotty
cloak.

'Your house is on fire, Mother
Ladybird! Fly away home to your
children!'

ANOTHER day, a big fat spider came in to shelter from the rain.

' Beg pardon, is this not Miss Muffet's?'

' Go away, you bold bad spider! Leaving ends of cobweb all over my nice clean house!'

SHE bundled the spider out at a window.

He let himself down the hedge with a long thin bit of string.

MRS. TITTLEMOUSE went on her way to a distant storeroom, to fetch cherry-stones and thistle-down seed for dinner.

All along the passage she sniffed, and looked at the floor.

'I smell a smell of honey; is it the cowslips outside, in the hedge? I am sure I can see the marks of little dirty feet.'

SUDDENLY round a corner, she met Babbitty Bumble—'Zizz, Bizz, Bizzz!' said the bumble bee.

Mrs. Tittlemouse looked at her severely. She wished that she had a broom.

'Good-day, Babbitty Bumble; I should be glad to buy some beeswax. But what are you doing down here? Why do you always come in at a window, and say Zizz, Bizz, Bizzz?' Mrs. Tittlemouse began to get cross.

'ZIZZ, Wizz, Wizzz!' replied Bab-bitty Bumble in a peevish squeak. She sidled down a passage, and disappeared into a storeroom which had been used for acorns.

Mrs. Tittlemouse had eaten the acorns before Christmas; the storeroom ought to have been empty.

But it was full of untidy dry moss.

MRS. TITTLEMOUSE began to pull out the moss. Three or four other bees put their heads out, and buzzed fiercely.

'I am not in the habit of letting lodgings; this is an intrusion!' said Mrs. Tittlemouse. 'I will have them turned out—' 'Buzz! Buzz! Buzzz!'— 'I wonder who would help me?' 'Bizz, Wizz, Wizzz!'

—'I will not have Mr. Jackson; he never wipes his feet.'

MRS. TITTLEMOUSE decided to leave the bees till after dinner.

When she got back to the parlour, she heard some one coughing in a fat voice; and there sat Mr. Jackson himself!

He was sitting all over a small rocking-chair, twiddling his thumbs and smiling, with his feet on the fender.

He lived in a drain below the hedge, in a very dirty wet ditch.

'HOW do you do, Mr. Jackson? Deary me, you have got very wet!'

'Thank you, thank you, thank you, Mrs. Tittlemouse! I'll sit awhile and dry myself,' said Mr. Jackson.

He sat and smiled, and the water dripped off his coat tails. Mrs. Tittlemouse went round with a mop.

H E sat such a while that he had to be asked if he would take some dinner?

First she offered him cherry-stones. 'Thank you, thank you, Mrs. Tittle-mouse! No teeth, no teeth, no teeth!' said Mr. Jackson.

He opened his mouth most unnecessarily wide; he certainly had not a tooth in his head.

THEN she offered him thistle-down seed—'Tiddly, widdly, widdly! Pouff, pouff, puff!' said Mr. Jackson. He blew the thistle-down all over the room.

'Thank you, thank you, thank you, Mrs. Tittlemouse! Now what I really—*really* should like—would be a little dish of honey!'

'I AM afraid I have not got any, Mr. Jackson,' said Mrs. Tittlemouse.

'Tiddly, widdly, widdly, Mrs. Tittlemouse!' said the smiling Mr. Jackson, 'I can *smell* it; that is why I came to call.'

Mr. Jackson rose ponderously from the table, and began to look into the cupboards.

Mrs. Tittlemouse followed him with a dish-cloth, to wipe his large wet footmarks off the parlour floor.

WHEN he had convinced himself that there was no honey in the cupboards, he began to walk down the passage.

'Indeed, indeed, you will stick fast, Mr. Jackson!'

'Tiddly, widdly, widdly, Mrs. Tittlemouse!'

FIRST he squeezed into the pantry.

'Tiddly, widdly, widdly? no honey? no honey, Mrs. Tittlemouse?'

There were three creepy-crawly people hiding in the plate-rack. Two of them got away; but the littlest one he caught.

THEN he squeezed into the larder.
Miss Butterfly was tasting the
sugar; but she flew away out of the
window.

'Tiddly, widdly, widdly, Mrs. Tittlemouse; you seem to have plenty of
visitors!'

'And without any invitation!' said
Mrs. Thomasina Tittlemouse.

THEY went along the sandy passage—'Tiddly widdly—' 'Buzz! Wizz! Wizz!'

He met Babbitty round a corner, and snapped her up, and put her down again.

'I do not like bumble bees. They are all over bristles,' said Mr. Jackson, wiping his mouth with his coat-sleeve.

'Get out, you nasty old toad!' shrieked Babbitty Bumble.

'I shall go distracted!' scolded Mrs. Tittlemouse.

SHE shut herself up in the nut-cellar while Mr. Jackson pulled out the bees-nest. He seemed to have no objection to stings.

When Mrs. Tittlemouse ventured to come out—everybody had gone away.

But the untidiness was something dreadful—'Never did I see such a mess—smears of honey; and moss, and thistledown—and marks of big and little dirty feet—all over my nice clean house!'

SHE gathered up the moss and the remains of the beeswax.

Then she went out and fetched some twigs, to partly close up the front door.

'I will make it too small for Mr. Jackson!'

SHE fetched soft soap, and flannel, and a new scrubbing brush from the storeroom. But she was too tired to do any more. First she fell asleep in her chair, and then she went to bed.

'Will it ever be tidy again?' said poor Mrs. Tittlemouse.

NEXT morning she got up very early and began a spring cleaning which lasted a fortnight.

She swept, and scrubbed, and dusted; and she rubbed up the furniture with beeswax, and polished her little tin spoons.

WHEN it was all beautifully neat
and clean, she gave a party to five
other little mice, without Mr. Jackson.

He smelt the party and came up the
bank, but he could not squeeze in at
the door.

SO they handed him out acorn-cupfuls of honeydew through the window, and he was not at all offended.

He sat outside in the sun, and said—
'Tiddly, widdly, widdly! Your very good health, Mrs. Tittlemouse!'

The Tailor of Gloucester

IN the time of swords and periwigs and full-skirted coats with flowered lappets—when gentlemen wore ruffles, and gold-laced waistcoats of paduasoy and taffeta—there lived a tailor in Gloucester.

He sat in the window of a little shop in Westgate Street, cross-legged on a table, from morning till dark.

All day long while the light lasted he sewed and snippeted, piecing out his satin and pompadour, and lutestring; stuffs had strange names, and were very expensive in the days of the Tailor of Gloucester.

But although he sewed fine silk for his neighbours, he himself was very, very poor—a little old man in spectacles, with a pinched face, old crooked fingers, and a suit of thread-bare clothes.

He cut his coats without waste, according to his embroidered cloth; they were very small ends and snippets that lay about upon the table—'Too narrow breadths for nought—except waistcoats for mice,' said the tailor.

One bitter cold day near Christmastime the tailor began to make a coat— a coat of cherry-coloured corded silk embroidered with pansies and roses, and a cream-coloured satin waistcoat— trimmed with gauze and green worsted chenille—for the Mayor of Gloucester.

The tailor worked and worked, and he talked to himself. He measured the silk, and turned it round and round, and trimmed it into shape with his

shears; the table was all littered with cherry-coloured snippets.

'No breadth at all, and cut on the cross; it is no breadth at all; tippets for mice and ribbons for mobs! for mice!' said the Tailor of Gloucester.

When the snow-flakes came down against the small leaded window-panes and shut out the light, the tailor had done his day's work; all the silk and satin lay cut out upon the table.

There were twelve pieces for the coat and four pieces for the waistcoat; and

there were pocket flaps and cuffs, and buttons all in order. For the lining of the coat there was fine yellow taffeta; and for the button-holes of the waistcoat, there was cherry-coloured twist. And everything was ready to sew together in the morning, all measured and sufficient—except that there was wanting just one single skein of cherry-coloured twisted silk.

The tailor came out of his shop at dark, for he did not sleep there at nights; he fastened the window and locked the door, and took away the key. No one lived there at night but little brown mice, and they run in and out without any keys!

For behind the wooden wainscots of all the old houses in Gloucester, there are little mouse staircases and secret trap-doors; and the mice run from house to house through those long narrow passages; they can run all over the town without going into the streets.

But the tailor came out of his shop,
and shuffled home through the snow.
He lived quite near by in College
Court, next the doorway to College
Green; and although it was not a big
house, the tailor was so poor he only
rented the kitchen.

He lived alone with his cat; it was
called Simpkin.

Now all day long while the tailor
was out at work, Simpkin kept house
by himself; and he also was fond of

the mice, though he gave them no
satin for coats!

'Miaw?' said the cat when the tailor
opened the door. 'Miaw?'

The tailor replied—'Simpkin, we
shall make our fortune, but I am worn
to a ravelling. Take this groat (which
is our last fourpence) and Simpkin,
take a china pipkin; buy a penn'orth
of bread, a penn'orth of milk and a
penn'orth of sausages. And oh, Simpkin, with the last penny of our four-

pence buy me one penn'orth of cherry-coloured silk. But do not lose the last penny of the fourpence, Simpkin, or I am undone and worn to a threadpaper, for I have NO MORE TWIST.'

Then Simpkin again said, ' Miaw ? ' and took the groat and the pipkin, and went out into the dark.

The tailor was very tired and beginning to be ill. He sat down by the hearth and talked to himself about that wonderful coat.

'I shall make my fortune—to be cut bias—the Mayor of Gloucester is to be married on Christmas Day in the morning, and he hath ordered a coat and an embroidered waistcoat—to be lined with yellow taffeta—and the taffeta sufficeth; there is no more left over in snippets than will serve to make tippets for mice—'

Then the tailor started; for suddenly, interrupting him, from the dresser at the other side of the kitchen came a

number of little noises—

Tip tap, tip tap, tip tap tip!

'Now what can that be?' said the Tailor of Gloucester, jumping up from his chair. The dresser was covered with crockery and pipkins, willow pattern plates, and tea-cups and mugs.

The tailor crossed the kitchen, and stood quite still beside the dresser, listening, and peering through his spectacles. Again from under a tea-cup, came those funny little noises—

Tip tap, tip tap, tip tap tip!

'This is very peculiar,' said the Tailor of Gloucester; and he lifted up the tea-cup which was upside down.

Out stepped a little live lady mouse, and made a curtsey to the tailor! Then she hopped away down off the dresser, and under the wainscot.

The tailor sat down again by the fire, warming his poor cold hands, and mumbling to himself—

'The waistcoat is cut out from peach-coloured satin—tambour stitch and rose-buds in beautiful floss silk. Was I

wise to entrust my last fourpence to
Simpkin? One-and-twenty button-holes
of cherry-coloured twist!'

But all at once, from the dresser,
there came other little noises:

Tip tap, tip tap, tip tap tip!

'This is passing extraordinary!' said
the Tailor of Gloucester, and turned
over another tea-cup, which was upside
down.

Out stepped a little gentleman mouse,
and made a bow to the tailor!

And then from all over the dresser came a chorus of little tappings, all sounding together, and answering one another, like watch-beetles in an old worm-eaten window-shutter—

Tip tap, tip tap, tip tap tip!

And out from under tea-cups and from under bowls and basins, stepped other and more little mice who hopped away down off the dresser and under the wainscot.

The tailor sat down, close over the

fire, lamenting—'One-and-twenty button-holes of cherry-coloured silk! To be finished by noon of Saturday: and this is Tuesday evening. Was it right to let loose those mice, undoubtedly the property of Simpkin? Alack, I am undone, for I have no more twist!'

The little mice came out again, and listened to the tailor; they took notice of the pattern of that wonderful coat. They whispered to one another about the taffeta lining, and about little mouse tippets.

And then all at once they all ran away together down the passage behind the wainscot, squeaking and calling to one another, as they ran from house to house; and not one mouse was left in the tailor's kitchen when Simpkin came back with the pipkin of milk!

Simpkin opened the door and bounced in, with an angry 'G-r-r-miaw!' like a cat that is vexed: for he hated the snow, and there was snow in his ears, and snow in his collar at

the back of his neck. He put down the loaf and the sausages upon the dresser, and sniffed.

'Simpkin,' said the tailor, 'where is my twist?'

But Simpkin set down the pipkin of milk upon the dresser, and looked suspiciously at the tea-cups. He wanted his supper of little fat mouse!

'Simpkin,' said the tailor, 'where is my TWIST?'

But Simpkin hid a little parcel privately in the tea-pot, and spit and growled at the tailor; and if Simpkin had been able to talk, he would have asked: 'Where is my MOUSE?'

'Alack, I am undone!' said the Tailor of Gloucester, and went sadly to bed.

All that night long Simpkin hunted and searched through the kitchen, peeping into cupboards and under the wainscot, and into the tea-pot where he had hidden that twist; but still he found never a mouse!

Whenever the tailor muttered and talked in his sleep, Simpkin said 'Miaw-ger-r-w-s-s-ch!' and made strange horrid noises, as cats do at night.

For the poor old tailor was very ill with a fever, tossing and turning in his four-post bed; and still in his dreams he mumbled—'No more twist! no more twist!'

All that day he was ill, and the next day, and the next; and what should become of the cherry-coloured coat? In the tailor's shop in Westgate Street the embroidered silk and satin lay cut out upon the table—one-and-twenty button-holes—and who should come to sew them, when the window was barred, and the door was fast locked?

But that does not hinder the little brown mice; they run in and out without any keys through all the old houses in Gloucester!

Out of doors the market folks went trudging through the snow to buy their

geese and turkeys, and to bake their Christmas pies; but there would be no Christmas dinner for Simpkin and the poor old Tailor of Gloucester.

The tailor lay ill for three days and nights; and then it was Christmas Eve, and very late at night. The moon climbed up over the roofs and chimneys, and looked down over the gateway into College Court. There were no lights in the windows, nor any sound in the houses; all the city of

Gloucester was fast asleep under the snow.

And still Simpkin wanted his mice, and he mewed as he stood beside the four-post bed.

But it is in the old story that all the beasts can talk, in the night between Christmas Eve and Christmas Day in the morning (though there are very few folk that can hear them, or know what it is that they say).

When the Cathedral clock struck twelve there was an answer—like an echo of the chimes—and Simpkin heard it, and came out of the tailor's door, and wandered about in the snow.

From all the roofs and gables and old wooden houses in Gloucester came a thousand merry voices singing the old Christmas rhymes—all the old songs that ever I heard of, and some that I don't know, like Whittington's bells.

First and loudest the cocks cried out: 'Dame, get up, and bake your pies!'

'Oh, dilly, dilly, dilly!' sighed Simpkin.

And now in a garret there were lights and sounds of dancing, and cats came from over the way.

'Hey, diddle, diddle, the cat and the fiddle! All the cats in Gloucester— except me,' said Simpkin.

Under the wooden eaves the starlings and sparrows sang of Christmas pies; the jack-daws woke up in the Cathedral tower; and although it was the middle of the night the throstles and robins

sang; the air was quite full of little twittering tunes.

But it was all rather provoking to poor hungry Simpkin!

Particularly he was vexed with some little shrill voices from behind a wooden lattice. I think that they were bats, because they always have very small voices—especially in a black frost, when they talk in their sleep, like the Tailor of Gloucester.

They said something mysterious that

sounded like—

'Buz, quoth the blue fly; hum, quoth the bee;
Buz and hum they cry, and so do we!'

and Simpkin went away shaking his ears as if he had a bee in his bonnet.

From the tailor's shop in Westgate came a glow of light; and when Simpkin crept up to peep in at the window it was full of candles. There was a snippeting of scissors, and snappeting of thread; and little mouse voices sang loudly and gaily—

' Four-and-twenty tailors
    Went to catch a snail,
    The best man amongst them
    Durst not touch her tail ;
    She put out her horns
    Like a little kyloe cow,
Run, tailors, run! or she'll have you all e'en now!'

Then without a pause the little mouse voices went on again—

' Sieve my lady's oatmeal,
    Grind my lady's flour,
    Put it in a chestnut,
    Let it stand an hour—'

'Mew! Mew!' interrupted Simpkin, and he scratched at the door. But the key was under the tailor's pillow, he

could not get in.

The little mice only laughed, and tried another tune—

> 'Three little mice sat down to spin,
> Pussy passed by and she peeped in.
> What are you at, my fine little men?
> Making coats for gentlemen.
> Shall I come in and cut off your threads?
> Oh, no, Miss Pussy, you'd bite off our heads!'

'Mew! Mew!' cried Simpkin. 'Hey diddle dinketty?' answered the little mice—

> 'Hey diddle dinketty, poppetty pet!
> The merchants of London they wear scarlet;
> Silk in the collar, and gold in the hem,
> So merrily march the merchantmen!'

They clicked their thimbles to mark the time, but none of the songs pleased Simpkin; he sniffed and mewed at the door of the shop.

'And then I bought
A pipkin and a popkin,
A slipkin and a slopkin,
All for one farthing—

and upon the kitchen dresser!' added the rude little mice.

'Mew! scratch! scratch!' scuffled Simpkin on the window-sill; while the little mice inside sprang to their feet, and all began to shout at once in little twittering voices: 'No more twist! No more twist!' And they barred up the window shutters and shut out Simpkin.

But still through the nicks in the shutters he could hear the click of thimbles, and little mouse voices sing-ing—

'No more twist! No more twist!'

Simpkin came away from the shop and went home, considering in his mind. He found the poor old tailor without fever, sleeping peacefully.

Then Simpkin went on tip-toe and took a little parcel of silk out of the tea-pot, and looked at it in the moon-light; and he felt quite ashamed of his badness compared with those good little mice!

When the tailor awoke in the morning, the first thing which he saw upon the patchwork quilt, was a skein of cherry-coloured twisted silk, and beside his bed stood the repentant Simpkin!

'Alack, I am worn to a ravelling,' said the Tailor of Gloucester, 'but I have my twist!'

The sun was shining on the snow when the tailor got up and dressed, and came out into the street with Simpkin running before him.

The starlings whistled on the chimney stacks, and the throstles and robins sang—but they sang their own little noises, not the words they had sung in the night.

'Alack,' said the tailor, 'I have my twist; but no more strength—nor time—than will serve to make me one

single button-hole; for this is Christmas Day in the Morning! The Mayor of Gloucester shall be married by noon— and where is his cherry-coloured coat?'

He unlocked the door of the little shop in Westgate Street, and Simpkin ran in, like a cat that expects something.

But there was no one there! Not even one little brown mouse!

The boards were swept clean; the little ends of thread and the little silk snippets were all tidied away, and gone from off the floor.

But upon the table—oh joy! the tailor gave a shout—there, where he had left plain cuttings of silk—there lay the most beautifullest coat and embroidered satin waistcoat that ever were worn by a Mayor of Gloucester.

There were roses and pansies upon the facings of the coat; and the waistcoat was worked with poppies and corn-flowers.

Everything was finished except just one single cherry-coloured button-hole, and where that button-hole was wanting there was pinned a scrap of paper with these words—in little teeny weeny writing—

NO MORE TWIST

And from then began the luck of the Tailor of Gloucester; he grew quite stout, and he grew quite rich.

He made the most wonderful waistcoats for all the rich merchants of

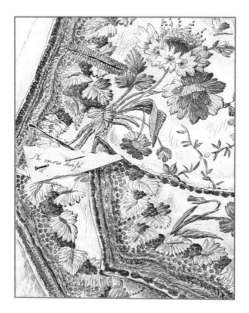

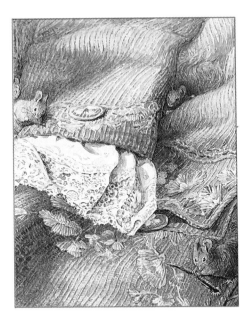

Gloucester, and for all the fine gentlemen of the country round.

Never were seen such ruffles, or such
embroidered cuffs and lappets! But his
button-holes were the greatest triumph
of it all.

The stitches of those button-holes
were so neat—*so* neat—I wonder how
they could be stitched by an old man
in spectacles, with crooked old fingers,
and a tailor's thimble.

The stitches of those button-holes were so small—*so* small—they looked as if they had been made by little mice!